DOCTOR · WHO

THE DARKSMITH LEGACY

THE ART OF WAR

BY MIKE TUCKER

Book
9

The Darksmith adventure continues online. Log on to
the website, enter the special codes from your book
and enjoy games and exclusive content about
The Darksmith Legacy.

www.thedarksmithlegacy.com

DOCTOR · WHO

THE DARKSMITH LEGACY

BBC CHILDREN'S BOOKS
Published by the Penguin Group
Penguin Books Ltd, 80 Strand, London, WC2R 0RL, England
Penguin Group (USA) Inc., 375 Hudson Street, New York 10014, USA
Penguin Books (Australia) Ltd, 250 Camberwell Road, Camberwell, Victoria 3124, Australia
(A division of Pearson Australia Group Pty Ltd)
Canada, India, New Zealand, South Africa
Published by BBC Children's Books, 2009
Text and design © Children's Character Books, 2009
Written by Mike Tucker
Cover illustration by Peter McKinstry
10 9 8 7 6 5 4 3 2 1
BBC logo © BBC 1996. Doctor Who logo © BBC 2004. TARDIS image © BBC 1963.
Licensed by BBC Worldwide Limited.
BBC, DOCTOR WHO (word marks, logos and devices), and TARDIS are trademarks of the
British Broadcasting Corporation and are used under licence.
ISBN: 978-1-40590-521-3
Printed in Great Britain by Clays Ltd, St Ives plc

Contents

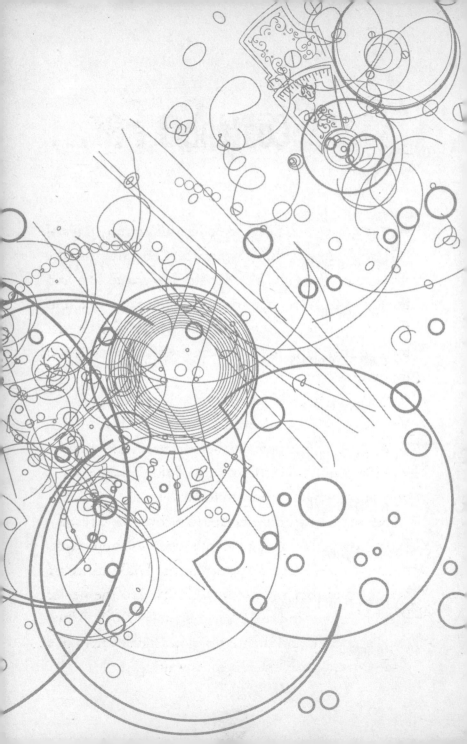

The Story So Far...

The Doctor has taken the powerful Eternity Crystal from the terrible Darksmith Collective on the planet Karagula. The Crystal can create life, and the Doctor knows it mustn't be allowed to fall into the wrong hands. The Darksmiths need the Crystal to fulfil their contract to create a terrible device for a mysterious client.

With the help of Gisella – the robot 'daughter' of Varlos, the Darksmith who created the Crystal – the Doctor tries to find out who the Darksmiths are working for. The people who commissioned the Crystal are the only ones who know how to destroy it.

But the Darksmiths manage to recover the Crystal – and to reprogramme Gisella so it seems she now works for them. The Doctor learns that the Darksmiths are due to hand over the Eternity Crystal and the device itself at a secret rendezvous on present day Earth. When the Darksmiths and their mysterious clients arrive in a disused warehouse, the Doctor is waiting...

Payment in Death

The warehouse roof had been removed, and the enormous space within was now open to the stars. And from the stars had come a ship to fill it – a huge warship. The Doctor held his breath as a door opened in the ship and a ramp descended.

A nightmare creature appeared in the blank opening of the doorway, and began to descend the ramp. Another followed, and another.

The Doctor stared in horror at the figures that appeared from inside the alien spaceship that had landed amongst the ruined brickwork and rusted pipes of the warehouse.

'Krashoks!'

The Doctor shook his head. 'That's not good… Not good at all.'

Six of the Krashok warriors had now emerged

from inside their ship. They looked like humans; at least they must have looked like humans once. Now they were an ugly mix of human being, robot and alien, mashed together like some strange jigsaw, each of them different from the next.

The Doctor had met them once – a long time ago, and a long way from Earth. He searched through his memory, trying to recall what he had learned about them.

They travelled the universe, searching for the most ferocious predators, the most successful fighters, taking the best bits from what they found and adding it to their own armoury. On the six Krashoks standing before him, the Doctor could recognize parts from nearly eleven different alien species. One had the huge, clawed paws of a Renevian tiger, another the muscular arms and poison tip darts of a Slitheen, yet another the thin, spike-encrusted legs of a Gappa. Sharp teeth, barbed tails and razor sharp spines from across the universe had been stitched onto the Krashoks' bodies, held in place by ugly robotic clamps.

The only unifying feature that identified them all as Krashoks was the hard ruff of bony scales that fanned out from behind their necks, the rough plates dotted with trophies and insignia of rank. The more senior the Krashok the more highly decorated the ruff.

It wasn't simply their external appearance that had been changed. The Doctor knew from unpleasant experience that the inside of any Krashok was just as much of a jumble of alien species. Lungs that helped them breath poison gas, hearts protected with bony plates, stomachs that allowed them to eat practically anything without getting ill.

Each of the Krashok warriors had gleaming metal helmets bolted to their heads, laser sights and flickering screens covering their right eyes. Backpacks bristling with weapons were slung across their shoulders, Dalek blasters, Cyberman guns, Rinteppi bazookas. The Krashok collected weapons from all over the galaxy. Anything to ensure that they were the superior fighting force in the universe, and that they had product to sell.

'Yes,' the Doctor murmured to himself. 'It makes sense. The Krashoks develop weapons, and then they start wars and sell the weapons that they've built to both sides. They are the ones who commissioned the Darksmiths in the first place!'

He shook his head angrily. The Krashoks were

about to engineer another war. With the Eternity Crystal finally recovered and Varlos's machine complete, the Krashoks would enable each side to keep raising their dead from the battlefield and the war would rage for centuries. An unending marketplace for the Krashoks and never mind who got caught in the crossfire and fallout.

The Doctor's jaw tightened. He had been through one war that had torn the universe apart. He wasn't about to sit by and let another one start.

He ducked down into the shadows of the warehouse as two more Krashoks emerged from the ship. These two were even more heavily armoured than their fellow warriors, their patchwork skins rough from the scars of battle, their neck ruffs encrusted with the insignia of rank. War Commanders. All Krashok campaigns were organized by two Commanders, each dealing with one of the opposing sides, both orchestrating the maximum carnage from behind the scenes.

As they appeared, the Darksmiths waiting for them bowed low. The Krashok leaders gave each other a sly grin, one revealing huge, yellowing tusks, the other gleaming metal fangs as their lips curled back.

'High Minister Drakon. A pleasure to see you again,' said one.

'I trust you have the Crystal?' hissed the other.

The High Minister pulled back the cowl of his cape, revealing his pale, skull-like face. With his skin pulled tight across his teeth it was impossible to tell if he was smiling or not.

'Commander Grelt. Commander Skraar,' he nodded at each in turn. 'But of course we have brought the Crystal. Would we have agreed to meet you on this... disagreeable planet if we had not?'

'Who knows what is in the mind of a Darksmith?' sneered Grelt. 'You have, after all, already left us waiting for millennia.'

'And that has lost us a lot of money, Drakon,' Skraar clumped down the ramp, towering over the frail body of the Darksmith. 'So where is the Crystal?'

Drakon waved a skeletal hand at Gisella. As the Doctor watched she stepped forward, holding out the case in her hands, snapping open the clasps and pulling open the lid.

The Krashok commanders hissed in pleasure, their patchwork faces lit up by the pale glow of the Eternity Crystal. Skraar reached out with a huge claw, but Drakon snapped the box shut sharply. Gisella looked at him, her pale face creasing with puzzlement. Skraar gave a snarl of displeasure, his hand reaching for the massive blaster that hung from his belt.

'Please, Commander,' Drakon held his hands up disarmingly. 'There's no need for any unpleasantness. The Crystal is here as agreed, but before you take possession of it there is the matter of payment to be discussed.'

Commander Grelt placed a huge armoured hand on the shoulder of his fellow Commander.

'Drakon has made a reasonable enough request. We should pay him what he is due.'

Skraar's hand relaxed from the butt of the blaster.

'Indeed.' He smiled. 'We have both waited long enough for this moment, a few more minutes will make no difference.'

From his hiding place the Doctor's mind was racing. In a matter of moments the Krashoks would have the Eternity Crystal inside their ship and this would all be over. He had to stop them!

He stared around at the crumbling ruins of the warehouse. High above him, rusting metal beams crisscrossed the grey of the night sky, all that remained of the collapsed roof. The Doctor's gaze flicked back and forth between the open roof and the gleaming bulk of the Krashok ship.

His eyes narrowed. The huge battlecruiser could have only just fit through the gap. If he could narrow that gap...

Pulling his sonic screwdriver from his jacket pocket he slipped his glasses onto his nose and squinted upwards, searching for weak points in the ruined roof.

Activity

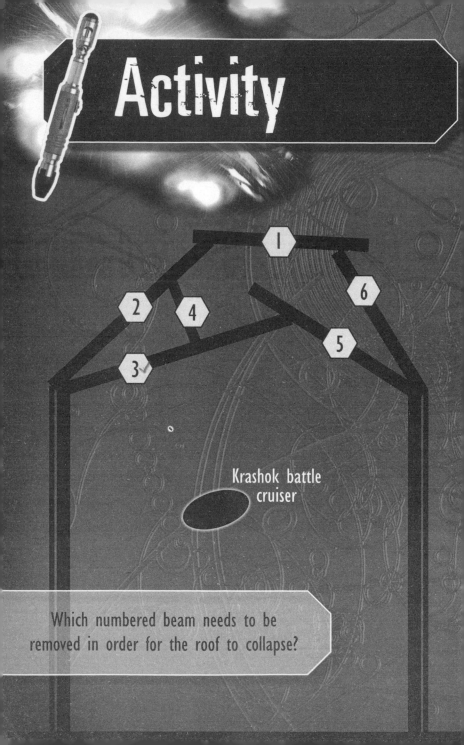

Krashok battle cruiser

Which numbered beam needs to be removed in order for the roof to collapse?

'A-ha!' he muttered. High above him half a dozen twisted beams met in a rust-encrusted jumble. If he could just get the frequency right…

He glanced over at where the Krashok and Darksmiths were talking. He frowned. Gisella was shuffling nervously from foot to foot, almost as if she was waiting for something. Or someone.

Two of the Krashoks had returned to their ship then re-emerged carrying a heavy chest between them. The deal was nearly done. He had to hurry.

He twisted a control on the body of the screwdriver and pressed down on the activation stud. A high sonic whine trilled out through the warehouse. From high above him a thin trickle of rust showered down onto the Doctor's face.

He brushed it away angrily. 'Wrong frequency,' he muttered, readjusting the screwdriver.

On the other side of the warehouse Drakon was reaching out for the chest, the smile on his skull-like face making him look even more like a grotesque, animated Hallowe'en mask.

Gritting his teeth against the harsh sonic vibrations, the Doctor continued to point the sonic screwdriver at the roof. The beams were starting to tremble, more and more rust flaking away. Several of the Krashok warriors had been alerted by the noise. If they spotted him…

'Come on!' said the Doctor under his breath. 'Bottom beam on the left – come on!'

At that moment Drakon lifted the lid of the chest, letting it fall open with a crash. His smile of greed faded and he looked up at the Krashok Commanders in puzzlement.

'But… there is nothing here.'

Grelt bared his yellow tusks. 'And nothing is exactly what you deserve.'

All six of the Krashok troopers unshouldered their weapons, aiming them at Gisella and the Darksmiths.

'A millennia of waiting, Drakon,' snarled Grelt. 'Hardly what you would call good customer service.'

He loomed over Gisella, reaching out for the box.

'You seriously expect us to pay your inflated fee for such gross inefficiency?'

Drakon made a futile attempt to pull him away. 'We have delivered what you asked for! We deserve payment!'

'Indeed.' Grelt turned on the Darksmith. 'Here is your payment.'

There was the harsh rattle of a gun. Smoke twisted from beneath Drakon's heavy robes. The

Darksmith's face contorted into an expression of pain and bewilderment, and he crashed to the ground with a wet thump. Despite the number of times that Drakon – or his minions – had tried to kill him, the Doctor couldn't help but feel some pity for the Darksmith. His years of plotting and waiting, come to this.

The other Darksmiths had turned to flee, but shots from half a dozen guns, from half a dozen planets, cut them down before they had barely moved.

Gisella stood amongst the carnage, her face impassive. The Krashoks surrounded her, Grelt holding out a clawed hand, the barrel of his gun pointed at Gisella's head.

'And now, Darksmith girl, you will give me the Crystal.'

Gisella held out the box.

Grelt took it with an unpleasant smile.

'Good. Now you die.'

Escape to the Past

The Doctor watched in horror as the Krashok Commander's finger tightened on the trigger of his gun. Suddenly, there was a tearing, metallic shriek from overhead.

Commander Grelt glanced up and his eyes widened in shock as the remains of the roof started to tumble down towards him. The Krashok troops scattered as metal beams and chunks of brickwork crashed to the ground around them. The Doctor threw himself to one side as a huge rusty pipe smashed into the pile of crates where he had been hiding, splintering them into a million pieces.

He rolled out into the chaos, snatching off his glasses and clambering to his feet. Gisella stood motionless, seemingly oblivious to the danger. The Doctor darted over to her. She looked up at him with a smile.

'I knew you'd be here.'

The Doctor caught her by the arm and pulled her to one side as a chunk of debris glanced off the hull of the Krashok ship with a deafening clang.

'So give me a good reason why I don't just leave you here,' the Doctor's voice was grim. 'If the Krashoks have possession of the Crystal...'

'But they don't!' Gisella caught hold of the Doctor's hand, her face beaming with joy. 'Don't you see! The Darksmith reprogramming didn't work. I've become more than just a machine, they can't just tell me what to do any more! That's why I made sure you knew the co-ordinates for this meeting.'

The Doctor's jaw dropped. 'So the Crystal that the Krashoks have just taken…'

'Is the copy that Varlos gave us when we met him in Paris. They don't know it, but the thing is useless to them.'

'Ha!' The Doctor picked up Gisella and swung her around. 'Genius! You're an absolute genius. Like father, like daughter.'

Another terrifying, grinding shriek made the Doctor stop and look up. The roof was in imminent danger of collapsing completely.

'I might have done rather too good a job of that.' He caught Gisella by the hand. 'Come on, the TARDIS is just over there.'

He turned, and found himself staring right down the barrel of Commander Skraar's blaster. The Krashok was limping badly, a ragged wound visible on his leg where he had been struck by falling masonry.

'I might have known that the Darksmiths were not to be trusted,' hissed the Commander painfully. 'Who are you? What is your species designation?'

'Er, I'm the Doctor.' The Doctor was backing away, keeping Gisella behind him. 'Just a local boy. Curiosity got the better of me, that's all. Nothing to do with any Darksmiths, me, oh no. Quite the opposite, in fact I was just leaving.'

'Just a local boy?' Skraar gave a humourless smile. 'With two heart signatures? I think not.'

'Ah well.' The Doctor shrugged. 'It's a fair cop. But I really think that we should go and talk somewhere a little less dusty. Very bad for the lungs.'

'I have the lungs of a Birostrop, and you are not going anywhere.'

'Really, I really think we should move. Right now.'

Skraar's finger tightened on the trigger of the blaster. 'Goodbye, local boy.'

The Doctor closed his eyes...

CRUNCH!

A huge chunk of brickwork and metal beams slammed into Skraar, crushing him into the ground.

The Doctor opened one eye and grimaced. 'I told him he shouldn't have stayed there. Some people just don't listen.'

He grabbed Gisella by the hand again and the two of them ran across the warehouse towards the waiting TARDIS. Behind them the Krashok troops scrambled desperately for the safety of their ship as the warehouse started to collapse in on itself.

The Doctor skidded to a halt as, through the chaos, he heard the low throb of engines starting up. He frowned. Surely he had done enough. Surely the ship could never make it into the air now. It was covered in tons of rubble.

Slowly the whine of the engines started to build.

Inside the Krashok ship Commander Grelt glared around the flight deck.

'Where is Commander Skraar?'

A trooper shot the Commander a nervous glance.

'He is not on board, sir.'

'Then find him!' bellowed Grelt.

The trooper hurried to a control console. 'The Commander's life register is red, sir.'

'What!' Grelt towered over the quivering trooper. 'Worthless cowardly scum like you survive and a Commander of the calibre of Skraar does not?!'

He turned to his pilot angrily.

'Get us airborn.'

'Impossible Commander.' The pilot struggled with the control column. 'The weight of rubble is too much.'

'Get this ship in the air, I say!'

'We have impact damage to the primary engine systems Commander. Even without the weight of rubble we cannot achieve escape velocity at this time.'

Grelt gave a bellow of rage. 'Is the secondary drive protocol undamaged?' he hissed.

'Yes, Commander, though the use of Dalek technology in Krashok cruisers is unproven in battle conditions.'

'Then it is time that it was tested.'

Grelt lowered his huge bulk into the command chair.

'All crew, prepare for emergency temporal shift.'

'What are they doing?' asked Gisella

'I don't know,' the Doctor sounded worried.

'Surely they can't take off like that?' Gisella stared at the mound of twisted metal that had buried the Krashok ship.

'No, they can't, but…'

The noise from the Krashok ship started to rise in pitch. Blue lightning flickered across the hull.

Gisella clamped her hands over her ears. 'What's happening?'

'No, no, no!' the Doctor cried out, with a flicker of blinding light the Kraskok ship vanished.

Gisella gaped at the hole in the rubble where the huge battle cruiser had once been.

'Where did it go?'

'They've temporal shifted! We've got to get back to the TARDIS! Quickly!'

'But why are we worried?' asked Gisella, as the Doctor bundled her inside the TARDIS. 'Surely it's good riddance to them, wherever they are?'

'It's not a question of *wherever* they are, it's a question of *whenever* they are.' The Doctor was dancing around the central console, stabbing at switches and twisting dials. 'They've only travelled in time, not in space. Emergency temporal drive. Dalek technology by the sound of it. The Krashoks must have looted it from a Skaro Saucer. Can't imagine the Daleks actually trading with them.'

'So the Krashoks are right here, right in this warehouse, or whatever stood or will stand where this warehouse is hundreds of years in the past or the future?'

'Well, give or take a few miles. They're travelling blind and on limited power. Ripples in the Time Vortex will have drifted them a bit. Time Winds too.'

'So how are we going to find them?'

'They will have left a faint trail through the Vortex. I've programmed the TARDIS scanners to follow that trail, so hopefully... Ah ha!' The Doctor clapped his hands triumphantly. 'Got 'em.'

Gisella joined him at the console, staring at the image in the scanner.

'They didn't have enough power to go very far.' The Doctor pointed at a flashing blip on the screen. 'Several hundred years or so in the past. Medieval London.'

'That's London?' Gisella asked incredulously. 'It's tiny!'

TARDIS
Data Bank

Medieval London

The population of Medieval London was about 80,000 people, a fraction of the population of the twenty-first century. Many of the families who settled in London during this period gave their names to districts — Clacton, Lincoln, Reading.

Most of the population was packed within the city walls, a layout influenced by the earlier Roman city plan, with only a small proportion living in the districts of Southwark and Westminster.

Westminster was separated from the City, with its own government. The City was ravaged by the Black Death in 1348. By 1350 almost half of the population had been killed.

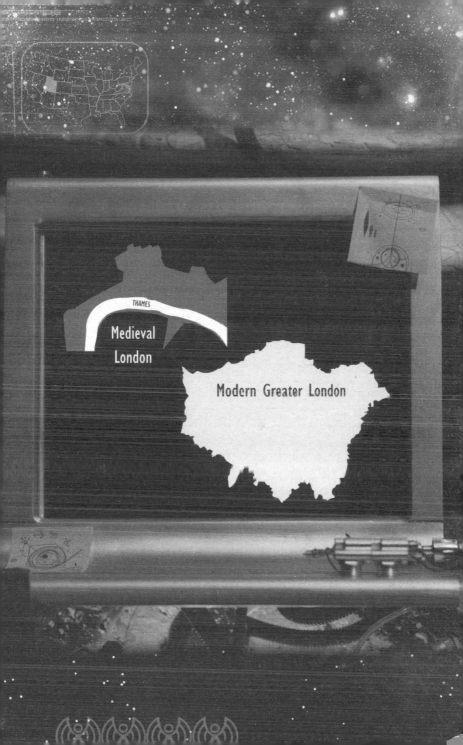

THAMES

Medieval
London

Modern Greater London

'And hopefully that should be easier for us to track them down.' The Doctor started programming the flight. 'We've not got much time.'

'Why?' Gisella looked puzzled.

'We have a small problem.' The Doctor looked at her apologetically. 'The Crystal that they now have is a copy, a fake. They can't possibly know that, so they'll install it in their machine anyway.'

'Isn't that exactly what we wanted? The machine won't work!'

'Oh, it'll work all right. Just not as they expect. Depending on how they've set it up, it could become a bomb. The Crystal will set up sympathetic resonance in the machine's reactor core. It'll destroy the Krashoks, their ship and the surrounding area. Maybe even the whole of whatever planet they're on when they try and operate it.'

Gisella's jaw dropped. 'A bomb? When were you going to tell me that particular fact!'

'Well you know how it is. Got busy. Had a game of death in a country house to deal with, the Dravidian Hive, my companion pretending to work with the Darksmiths…'

'Hey! I was trying to help!'

'And right now we've got a planet to save. Hang

on, Gisella! This might be a bit rough!'

The Doctor threw a switch and the TARDIS hurled itself into the Vortex.

Bard Company

The sun was low on the horizon, casting long, hazy shadows over the snow-flecked fields. Oswald pulled his cloak around him and shivered, cursing his luck at being out in the cold instead of sat in front of a roaring fire with a cup of mead.

It was his own fault. He should have known better than to pick a fight with the biggest blacksmith in the village, particularly over a girl.

Oswald smiled. She had been a very pretty girl, though. And she had taken quite a shine to him with his songs and his jokes. A shame that the blacksmith had his eye on her as well. In retrospect, telling the blacksmith that he had the face of an ox and the personal hygiene of a herd of swine might not have been the best course of action. Still, the fight, and his miraculous escape, would make a good song or poem.

Oswald picked up his lute, shaking the snow from it. It wasn't just his body that needed warmth, his lute was hardly going to sound its best sodden and damp. He gave a deep sigh and stared out across the frozen fields. He needed shelter for the night. It was just a question of where.

Going back to the village he had just left was probably not a good idea. However attractive Lily the barmaid might be, the blacksmith had made it perfectly clear what would happen to him if he set foot there again. That left him two options if he was to avoid spending a night in the open. London, or Sir Howard Blackheart's castle.

In the distance, beyond the glimmering ribbon of water that was the Thames, he could see smoke from the chimneys of Westminster rising into the pale November air. London had always been his ultimate goal. But he had hoped to arrive there looking somewhat less bedraggled. He looked down at his soaked and mud-splattered cloak. To be the talk of the town, the most famous bard in England required his arrival to be conducted with a little more style, a little more dignity.

That left him with Sir Howard Blackheart's castle. A night's entertainment in return for food and lodging. A modest, but memorable performance for the Lord and his followers. The castle was just visible through the hazy air, its high walls and fluttering pennants silhouetted against the setting sun.

Oswald shivered again, though not from the cold. Back at the inn there had been stories, rumours of a plague sweeping through the men and women that worked Sir Blackheart's lands. Of a death that struck healthy men down where they stood. A peddler who had fled the village had told of lights in the night sky, of lightning and a mighty wind, of the very land itself cracking open. Oswald crossed himself hurriedly. If there were demons about then he had no desire to be out in the night with them.

Gathering up his belongings Oswald scrambled to his feet and set off towards the distant castle. If he kept up a good pace then he should be able to reach the gates by nightfall.

His path led him down the hillside and through a small copse of trees, their leafless branches casting long shadows across the frozen earth. Out of the sunlight and in the shadow of the wood the cold was biting and Oswald was glad of his heavy cloak.

He looked up in alarm as, with a flutter of wings and chorus of rasping cries, a flock of crows took flight from the branches of one of the taller trees. Oswald stopped. The crows had been frightened by someone. Or something.

With his heart pounding, he strained to listen for sounds of movement in the darkening wood. Confronting the blacksmith again suddenly didn't seem like such a bad option after all.

Oswald shook his head. 'There's nothing here,' he muttered to himself. 'You've been taken in by peasant rumours, that's all. The great storyteller frightened by the camp fire tale of a farmer with an overactive imagination.'

Convincing himself that the crows had been disturbed by a squirrel or bird of prey, Oswald set off through the wood once more, though his pace was somewhat faster than it had been.

A sudden noise made him stop again. A holly bush, its branches heavy with berries, was starting to sway, its leaves rustling as they brushed against a moss laden oak tree. Above him the branches of the tree were starting to move, slowly at first but with increasing violence. Oswald stared in panic. The air had been still and quiet, there had been no breath of wind, so what was rustling the leaves?

A terrifying trumpeting started to fill the air and Oswald had to cover his face with his cloak as the ghostly wind suddenly swirled dead leaves around him. Blue light illuminated the woodland as the noise reached fever pitch and then, with a sudden 'thump' there was silence once more.

Oswald stared open mouthed at the thing that had appeared before him. It was a tall blue box, its wooden surface scarred and weathered. Tentatively Oswald approached. It was certainly no demon. There was a low hum coming from it, like the sound of bees in their hive.

He leapt back as a door on the side of the box sprang open and a tall thin man in a long, heavy coat sprang out, arms outstretched.

'There we go Gisella! Right on the button. Ah – smell that air! Nice crisp, medieval air, no hydrocarbons, no dichlorodifluoromethane, no artificial flavourings. Just damp earth, pine needles and freshly fallen snow.'

'Er, Doctor.' A small, dark haired child had also appeared from the box and was staring straight at Oswald.

'Hm, yes, what?' The man spun around. 'Oh...'

For a moment Oswald just stood there, unable to think what to say or do.

Then he collapsed in a dead faint.

Commander Grelt pushed his way through the thick cobwebs that hung in the tunnel, grimacing with distaste as the sticky strands clung to his armour. The walls of the narrow passageway were slimy and thick with roots and the only light came from spluttering candles in crudely gouged alcoves.

Grelt could not believe how primitive these people were, or how they had ever managed to survive long enough to develop any sort of technology. But survive they had, and if he and his men were to survive as well then unfortunately he was in need of their help.

The temporal shift had left his ship stranded. The long flight to Earth, coupled with the damage from the collapsing warehouse had left them dangerously low on power. The Dalek technology needed to hurl the saucer back through time had all but drained that power. His technicians had estimated that once repairs were completed they would need seventy-two hours before their energy banks were recharged and they were in a position to move the ship again. Seventy-two hours trapped in the history of this miserable backwater planet.

Grelt hissed in displeasure. The death of his fellow commander had left him in a foul temper. His troopers were keeping their distance from him, wary of the boiling anger that could erupt at any moment. The primitives of this world had already borne the brunt of that anger, more than a dozen dead within minutes of their landing. It had been Jorak, his Sergeant-at-Arms who had had the good sense to restrain him, pointing out that with their limited numbers they were vulnerable. The primitives might be poorly armed but they had numbers on their side. Better to enlist their help than to incur their anger.

Grelt allowed himself a smile of pride. Jorak would make a good leader. When the time was right he would ensure that the badge of Commander was added to his insignia of rank.

Krashok Military Insignia

Krashoks have:

- Commander
- Sergeant-at-Arms
- Squad Leader
- Pilot
- Trooper

Troopers who distinguish themselves in military campaigns are awarded their medals at a ceremony knows as 'The Branding of the Brave'. Here they kneel before their superiors and their medals are clamped into place on the ruff of bone around their necks. As they climb the ladder of rank, more insignia are added to the ruff.

Krashoks disgraced in battle have their insignias removed by laser, the scars forever branding them as cowards.

The highest honour that a Krashok can receive is 'The Order of Trekanaa', named after the Krashok Commander who successfully instigated the Millennium War, a mighty conflict that raged for thousands of years, and made the Krashok nation rich.

Commander

Sergeant

Pilot

The tunnel started to widen. A ragged veil of filthy cloth had been strung from the walls, concealing the far end. Grelt swept it aside and stepped through.

His nose wrinkled in distaste as the smell of burning herbs and incense caught at the back of his throat. A fire blazed in a pit scraped in the floor of the dingy cave, the carcass of some animal suspended on a crude spit.

Sensors in Grelt's headset switched his display to infrared and he glared around impatiently.

'You said you had something important to tell me, primitive,' he bellowed. 'So show yourself and tell me, and stop wasting my time.'

'Time, my Lord?' There was a rasping cackle from the far side of the cavern and a shuffling figure emerged from the gloom. 'I would have thought that one who travels in a manner such as yourself would have no shortage of time?'

Grelt glared at the wizened figure that stood before him. Amongst all the primitives this woman seemed to show no fear. Indeed she seemed to have knowledge far beyond that of her fellow creatures. They feared her, mumbling about witchcraft. Grelt had no such fears, but the woman had a gift, there was no denying that, and that gift was of use to him.

'There is more than a little of the Carrionite about you, woman,' he growled. 'Now, what news is so important that it drags me to your stinking hovel?'

'I apologize that my humble abode is not to your liking, my Lord Grelt.' She smiled, revealing crooked yellowing teeth. 'But my news may be more to your taste. Another has arrived.'

'Another? What do you mean?'

'Another from the future.'

'Impossible!' snarled Grelt.

'The manner of his arrival was not as grand as yours, but he is from the future, nonetheless.' The witch turned, sniffing at the roasting carcass. 'He hides his power beneath the trappings of a fool, but he is a danger to you, my Lord. He has already dispatched one of your number.'

Grelt sucked in a breath. The man from the warehouse. The stranger who had been responsible for the death of Commander Skraar. The one who had called himself the Doctor. Grelt had watched the video feed from Skraar's helmet over and over until every detail of the man's face was imbedded in his memory. He had thought that he had been cheated of his revenge, but now...

Grelt's face cracked into a vicious smile. 'Where can I find him?'

Unexpected Guests

Oswald woke with a start to find the girl from the box looking down at him with a smile on her face.

'Doctor,' she called. 'He's awake.'

The tall thin man came over, beaming down at him. 'How you feeling? Bit of a sore head? You went down with a good old thump. Gave us quite a fright!'

'I gave you quite a fright?' Oswald struggled to sit up. 'I think you are mistaken, sir. The fright was all mine.'

He looked around, his jaw dropping as he took in the room around him.

'May God preserve us. Where am I?'

'This is the TARDIS.' The girl helped him to his feet. Despite her size her grip was strong. 'My name is Gisella, that's the Doctor.'

Oswald gave a low bow, immediately regretting it as the world swirled around him.

The Doctor held out a steadying arm. 'Steady as you go sunshine. You've a mild concussion, that's all. You'll be right as rain in no time.'

Oswald felt the back of his head gingerly. There was a bump there. 'You are a man of medicine, then?'

'Well, sort of,' the Doctor grinned.

'And this is your ship, you say.' Oswald stared around in awe. ''Tis like no ship I have ever seen.'

'Well, yes. Not like your normal ship mind you, I'm not quite sure how best to explain…'

'Surely this cannot be the blue box I saw appear in a rush of wind?' Oswald wandered over to the open door and peered out in amazement.

'Well, like I said, it's a little tricky to explain,' said the Doctor

Oswald stepped out into the wood. The box was still a box. He walked round it once, returned to the door and stepped inside once more.

'But this is magnificent!' He clapped his hands and gave a cry of joy. 'A box that travels on a breeze of its own making, indeed, that travels through the very air itself! A wondrous engine the size of which is confounding to the mind, being larger within, and you, two travellers from beyond this land. Please, sir, I beg of you, you must tell me of your home. You must tell me of your travels!'

The Doctor and Gisella exchanged astonished looks.

Oswald bowed again, all hint of a headache banished. 'Sir. Madam. I am Oswald of Devizes, minstrel, storyteller, juggler and magician. Teller of tales and singer of songs. I have seen sights that mortal man has only dreamed of, witnessed great battles and mighty deeds, travelled the length and breadth of England and the Celtic lands in search of stories that I can weave into verse and you have given me the makings of a story so fantastic, so majestic that my name will be renowned throughout the kingdom.'

'Well, self promotion certainly doesn't seem to be your problem.' The Doctor ran his hand through his hair. 'Minstrel, eh... Well, yes, I love a good singsong me, but you might want to be a bit sparing with the truth, Oswald. It's the Middle Ages after all. Blue boxes appearing from nowhere. Rooms that are bigger on the inside. Going to be a bit difficult to swallow isn't it?'

'Ah, but the tale I shall spin will hold them

entranced.' Oswald could already see the faces of his adoring public. 'They shall be astounded by my bravery.'

'Says the man who dropped in a dead faint the moment he clapped eyes on us.' Gisella folded her arms and regarded him with amusement.

Oswald raised a dismissive hand. 'Ah, that is when I thought you to be the demons supposed to have laid waste to Lord Blackheart's serfs. You are no demons, for if you were then surely you would have left me where I lay.'

'Demons?' The Doctor and Gisella exchanged a worried glance. 'What demons?'

'A peasant's tale, nothing more. Demons that supposedly arrived last night in a storm, a plague that cut down the workers in the fields without sign of pox. A tawdry tale. Ramblings that have more to do with ale than art, I'll wager.'

'Oswald, this is important.' The Doctor's voice had taken on an urgency. 'Do you know where these demons are? Where they arrived?'

Oswald gulped. 'Then the tale is not fiction? There truly are demons?'

'Oh yes. Bad to the bone. And if I'm going to stop them then you need to show me where they are.'

'But the plague…' Oswald backed away, panic rising in his chest.

'There is no plague.' The Doctor caught him by the shoulders. 'Oswald, I can't explain everything to you, but if you help me, if you *trust* me, then I will make sure that when this is all over you will have the most *fantastic* story to tell. Deal?'

Oswald nodded.

'Good man,' the Doctor beamed. 'Now, where can I find these demons?'

'They were meant to have appeared in the land of Sir Howard Blackheart.'

'Sir Howard Blackheart eh?' The Doctor rubbed his chin. 'Never heard of him. How far is this castle?'

'No more than a mile. I had hoped to take shelter there before your box interrupted my journey.'

'Right then! A brisk walk should give us a good appetite for dinner. The nobility always put on a good spread. Come on Oswald, Gisella. Allons-y!'

Sergeant Jorak marched along corridors practically stripped of equipment. The ship was dangerously low on power and all repairs were taking place in Blackheart's castle, his servants doing the lifting and heavy carrying that would normally be done by the service robots. The robots themselves were powered down, useless until the ship was at full operating capacity. The crew was focused on getting the battle cruiser spaceworthy again. Their Commander, however, had other things on his mind. Grelt had summoned him to the armoury and Jorak was certain that the Commander wasn't meeting him there to admire its contents.

He punched his security code into the armoury door and stepped into the vault. Grelt was already inside. Jorak watched as his Commander strode across the huge room and snatched a Magnatarri pulse rifle. The Magnatarri weren't renowned for their subtlety. The pulse rifle was a devastating weapon.

Grelt snapped home a magazine, then threw the rifle over his shoulder, aiming at an insignia on the far wall. Jorak could see his finger tightening on the trigger.

'Commander Grelt?' Jorak's voice cut through the quiet of the armoury. Grelt let the rifle drop.

'Jorak. Good. Select a weapon.'

'Sir?'

'He is here! The alien from the warehouse, the one who calls himself Doctor, the one responsible for Skraar's death!'

'Impossible!'

'That witch in the cavern has seen him, sensed him, whatever it is she does. He's here, Jorak!'

'Sir!' Jorak's voice was harsh. Grelt glared at him.

'What is it, Sergeant?'

Jorak took a deep breath. Grelt was notoriously unforgiving when his subordinates disagreed with him. 'With respect, sir, the psychic abilities of the primitive woman are unreliable at best, her intentions even more so. This could be a trap.'

Grelt's eyes narrowed. 'She wouldn't dare.'

'We are too few in number to risk open confrontation. The repairs are taking every available man. The warriors of the man Blackheart are at your command. Why expose yourself to danger when they can search for this Doctor for us? If he is here then they can bring him to us. If it is a ruse…'

'Then the witch will live to regret it.' Grelt placed the rifle back in its rack. 'Good advice again, Jorak. Have Blackheart meet me in his great hall. Tell him to have his best men ready.'

'Yes sir.'

'If the Doctor is here he is not going to escape again, Jorak. He will die!'

Village of Fear

The sun was well below the horizon when the Doctor, Gisella and Oswald entered the village. The battlements of Sir Howard Blackheart's castle loomed in the distance, dark and brooding against the blood-red clouds caught in the dying light of the day.

Children ran from the Doctor and his companions, calling for their mothers. Wives clung to their husbands. All around them the faces that stared back were full of hostility and fear.

'I have played to friendlier crowds in my time,' murmured Oswald, casting a wary look at the pitchforks and scythes clutches in the hands of the villagers.

'They're terrified,' said the Doctor. 'Terrified and angry. Never a good combination.'

As they walked towards the centre of the village a crowd started to build, following them at a distance. Gisella caught hold of the Doctor's hand. He gave it a reassuring squeeze.

As they approached the village square a tall, bearded man stepped into their path.

'Who are you, strangers? What do you want here?'

The Doctor stepped forward. 'I'm the Doctor. I'm here to help.'

'A doctor, you say? What makes you think we are in need of doctors?'

'Last night. Something happened. Something came here. Something you didn't understand.'

The bearded man shook his head. 'I don't know what you mean.'

'Demons. Demons that arrived in a storm, that killed your friends.'

'This one has had a touch too much mead, methinks.' The man raised his voice to the crowd. "Demons," he says. Perhaps we have found our new village idiot.'

He gave a forced laugh, dry and humourless. No one else laughed.

'Why aren't they admitting it?' whispered Gisella. 'Why pretend it never happened?'

54

'They're terrified of being shunned by their neighbours,' said the Doctor. 'Scared that if word gets out that the village has a plague or some kind of demonic possession then no one will buy their goods or trade with them. The entire village will be quarantined, or worse…'

Oswald stepped forward, addressing the crowd. 'My friends, we know of your blight. Less than two hours ago in an ale house not two miles from here the tale of your village's misfortune has been told. A peddler who saw the lights in the sky with his own eyes.'

A frightened murmur swept through the villagers. 'I knew we shouldn't have let him go,' hissed one. 'We should have silenced his wagging tongue.'

'These strangers will bring the might of the king's whole army down upon us.'

The crowd started to mutter, closing in on the Doctor, Gisella and Oswald.

'Listen to me!' The Doctor had to shout to be heard. 'I can help. The lights that you saw, the demons that attacked you. I know what they are, I know how to stop them!'

'He knows what they are!' roared the bearded man. 'A man who consorts with demons! Enough,

I say! We have suffered enough.'

A stone thrown from the crowd landed at the Doctor's feet.

He danced backwards as more and more stones started to shower down around them.

The Doctor tried to grab hold of Gisella's hand as he struggled to reach for his psychic paper. If he could just convince the villagers that he was here to help. Oswald cried out in pain as a missile caught him on his shoulder.

A rock glanced off the Doctor's head, sending him reeling into the mud. He was aware of Gisella calling his name, of the girl turning on the crowd, her face darkening angrily.

'No, Gisella, don't,' he cried weakly, reaching out for her.

Too late he watched as Gisella reached out for the nearest villagers, grasping them by their tunics. Their fellows watched in amazement as she hoisted the two men high above her head, then hurled them over the crowd. They landed in a nearby cart in a cloud of hay and splintered wood.

Another villager lunged at her with a pitchfork. Gisella neatly sidestepped, clubbing the man to the floor with her elbow, quickly snatching the pitchfork from his hands.

To the astonishment of the watching crowd she twisted the prongs of the pitchfork into a neat knot and threw the now useless weapon to one side.

The crowd stared at her open mouthed.

The Doctor staggered to his feet, trying to clear his swimming head.

'I really don't think that that is going to have helped.'

A single word sprang from the lips of the man with the beard.

'Witch!'

The crowd surged forward.

The chapel in Sir Howard Blackheart's castle was a modest affair, a small room in the eastern wing, a single window of coloured glass designed to catch the rays of the morning sun, the only source of natural light. Now, with the light of the day gone, and a winter's night making its icy fingers felt, the chapel was cold and sinister, the dozens of candles that hung from the ceiling barely illuminating the shadows between the pillars.

Sir Howard stood in front of the altar, staring at the stone tomb in the centre of the chapel. He reached out a pale hand and touched the stone face of the carving in front of him: a young woman, arms folded across her chest, a posy of delicate stone flowers clasped in her carved hands.

The creatures from the sky had promised him much. They had spoken of a magical device that could revive the bodies of those killed in battle. They promised him an army of men that could never be killed.

He smiled. Reason enough to help these demons from hell, but he had another. There was one specific person that he wished to see revived from the dead. And if he did as these demons wished…

The door to the hall swung open gingerly. Sir Howard turned and watched as Sir Robert Markham, his Knight-at-Arms, his champion, crossed the chapel and knelt before him.

'You summoned me, my Lord.'

'Indeed, Sir Robert. Lord Grelt has need of you and your knights.'

Markham crossed himself clumsily and glanced around the dark corners.

'The demon is here? On holy ground?'

'No.' With a smile Sir Howard pulled a gleaming silver box from inside his robes. 'He spoke to me on this. He calls it "a communicator". I commune with him, Markham!'

'Sire, may I speak openly?'

The knight's face had an unfamiliar expression. With a start Sir Howard realized that it was fear. He nodded.

'These, demons, these… things. Is it wise to give them our trust? You give them shelter, you let your servants wait upon them but what do they offer in return? Weapons of the kind that struck down our people in the fields?'

'No, Markham. The demons intend to keep their weapons safely locked away in their metal machine.' Sir Howard picked up an ornate candlestick from the altar. 'We do not possess enough wealth to trade with them. But then, I never had call to believe that my family fortune would be needed to barter with creatures from beyond the stars.'

'Then why do we suffer their insolence, sire? Their bearing is not of nobility, but of savagery and tyranny. They treat us like worms.'

'I have made a bargain with them, and I will not come from this arrangement empty-handed.' Sir Howard placed the candlestick back on the altar, his hand falling to the carved stone face once more. 'Now, the Lord Grelt requests that you attend him in the great hall.'

Markham rose to his feet. 'I too regret the passing of the Lady Beatrice,' he said quietly. 'But I do not trust these creatures from another world. They have beguiled you with promises of their magic. No good will come of it.'

'That is enough, Sir Robert!' Blackheart's voice hardened. 'Grelt has need of your services. You will do as he asks. Disobey him and you disobey me.'

'Sire.' Markham bowed then turned and left the chapel, the swishing of his cloak making the candles flicker.

Blackheart stared down at the stone face of his dead wife. 'The Eternity Crystal,' he murmured. He had to believe in the promises of these creatures. He had to.

The Doctor struggled to reach Gisella as a dozen pairs of hands hoisted her roughly into the air.

'This isn't helping anyone!' he shouted.

No one listened to him. Ignoring the Doctor and Oswald the crowd bundled Gisella away, the sheer weight of numbers stopping her from breaking free. To one side of the square the Doctor could see a crudely constructed ducking stool by the village pond. They were going to be tried as witches!

The crowd thrust her into the roughly made chair. The Doctor struggled to reach her but hands held him firm. 'Listen to me. I'm the only one who can help you. If the Krashoks activate their Eternity Device then this entire area will be devastated. I'm your only chance.'

'Don't worry, Warlock!' bellowed the man with the beard. 'We'll let you have your turn soon enough!'

The Doctor stared down helplessly as the chair was hoisted into the air with Gisella struggling to free herself from her bonds. The water wouldn't kill her. It would merely confirm what the villagers thought, that she was supernatural, a witch. He could see her readying herself to use all her strength. When the villagers found out that she wasn't human they would tear her to pieces...

The chair swung out over the pond.

The man with the beard raised his hand.

Hunting Party

'Stop!'

A small man in the robes of a friar was running across the square.

'What in God's name do you think you are doing?' The friar was red faced with exertion and anger. 'Hasn't there been enough death in this village?' he puffed. 'Haven't there been enough innocents taken to God? She's a child! Surely you can see that she is just a child!'

The crowd backed away, shamefaced, as if suddenly aware of how small and vulnerable the so-called witch that they had caught actually looked. A woman started sobbing.

The man with the beard pushed his way to the friar, mumbling his explanations. 'But the girl has the strength of ten men. The man claims knowledge of the demons. Their clothes and manner are strange. Please Father, I have already lost a son, I have no wish for more misfortune to befall our village…'

'Then perhaps we should listen to these strangers.' The friar's voice was scathing. 'If this man claims to have knowledge of the demons that have beset us then perhaps we should make use of that knowledge instead of condemning him for it.'

The friar pushed past the villagers to where the Doctor was helping Gisella from the chair.

'Is the girl unharmed?'

'The girl is fine,' snapped Gisella, shaking off the last of her bonds.

'Thank you.' The Doctor smiled warmly at the little man. 'Thank you very much, Father…?'

'Meadows. You must forgive Jacob and the others.' The friar scowled at the man with the beard. 'We have had… troubles of late.'

'Yes,' said the Doctor ruefully. 'We heard…'

'Who are you?'

'I'm the Doctor, this is Gisella, and the young gentleman over there is Oswald of Devizes, a minstrel.'

The friar gave a rather disapproving look at the young bard, who was agitatedly checking that his lute had survived the rough handling.

'A Doctor, a child and a minstrel. Strange travelling companions.'

'Oh, I think that you have seen a lot stranger things over the past few hours.'

'Which you claim knowledge of?'

The Doctor reached into his pocket and removed his psychic paper. 'Special Envoy from the King. We're a sort of secret royal investigation team. Demons, witches, unexplained plagues of newts, that sort of thing…'

The friar took the paper and peered at it. 'And the bard?'

'Documents it all for us, official sonnets, poems in triplicate, you know what its like with paperwork… Now, these demons of yours. Sorry to be pushy, but they arrived in a lightning storm I hear. Rushing wind, terrible noise. All fairly routine, but I would like to see where they landed.'

The friar handed the Doctor back his psychic paper and crossed himself. 'You will find none here who will go near the place. Seven ventured out into the fields when the storm had abated. Six died where they stood. One still suffers the torments that the demons inflicted upon him.'

'You've got a survivor?' The Doctor looked at

him in astonishment. 'Well why didn't you say so!'

The friar shook his head. 'There is nothing that can be done.'

'Not by you perhaps. But I'm the Doctor! Now show me!'

Markham swung open the huge wooden doors of the great hall and strode into the room, ignoring the contemptuous glances of the gathered Krashoks.

The great hall of the castle was huge and impressive, a vast stone space, its walls hung with tapestries, a great fire blazing in a massive fireplace. Usually a long table piled high with expensive silver plates and candlesticks stretched along its entire length, with Sir Blackheart seated proudly at one end.

But now the furniture was heaped into an untidy pile in a corner, and unfamiliar alien shapes littered the flagstone floor, the aliens that fashioned them prodding and poking at the machinery with strange equipment. Blackheart's servants staggered amongst them, worked to the point of exhaustion by their demonic overseers.

Grelt stood at the fireplace, his huge bulk huddled over the roaring flames. At the sound of the doors he turned, smiling that crocodilian smile of his.

'Ah, Sir Blackheart's champion. Good. I have a task for you.'

'A task? You mean there is something that we primitives are good for after all?'

'A few things, yes. We are in need of more willing helpers. They fetch and carry well, but their strength is somewhat lacking.'

Markham looked about at the grubby and exhausted servants.

'You have taken all that we have.'

'Then you will need to fetch more. From the village. Strong men to carry and women and children to re-attach the drive circuits in the engine ducts. Slim bodies, Sir Knight, small enough to crawl through the narrowest of spaces.'

Markham shot the Krashok a look of distaste. 'If you need the help of the people from the village then perhaps it was a mistake to have killed so many of them.'

Grelt stepped down from the fireplace, towering over Markham. 'You don't like us, do you, Sir Knight?'

'It is no matter whether I like or dislike you. I do my Lord's bidding, and he bids me attend you.'

'And like a good soldier you follow orders,' Grelt smiled. 'But I can see in your eyes that you would kill me if you could. That you think we are unwelcome guests. Unwelcome save for our weapons.'

Markham's eyes dropped to the gun at Grelt's belt. The Krashok followed his gaze. 'Yes. You are a soldier. And you know what advantage a weapon such as ours would give you. Well perhaps, Sir Knight we can trade…'

Markham looked up at the Krashok quizzically.

'I have a challenge for you, Sir Knight. A quarry that might test even your mettle.' Grelt grinned.

He turned towards the wall, stabbing at controls on his armour with his claws. A beam of light sprang from his helmet, casting an image on the stone. Markham stared in disbelief, the image was moving. He moved towards it, mesmerized by the face of the thin-faced man that now stared back at him from the castle wall.

'Study him well. He may not look like much but he has already put paid to one of my most trusted Commanders.'

Markham frowned. 'But he is just a man, surely with your weapons, your powers…'

'Oh, this one is cunning. He calls himself the Doctor. Bring him to me, Sir Knight. Bring him to me and I will take that as a most generous payment.'

Markham turned, his eyes straying once more to the gun at Grelt's belt. Remembering how the demon had struck down the villagers in the field without even touching them.

The Krashok smiled. 'Do we have an agreement?'

Markham nodded. 'You shall have this Doctor before the night is out.'

Friar Meadows led the Doctor and his companions to the small church on the far side of the village square. He pushed open a wooden door and ushered them into the cool, calm dark.

Seven beds lined the walls of the tiny church. Six of those beds held bodies swathed in shrouds, the final one held a twisting, writhing figure. The Doctor hurried over. In the bed lay a young man, no more than seventeen years old. His face was twisted in pain, sweat pouring from his brow.

'Saints preserves us.' Oswald went pale. 'He has the plague.'

'Rubbish.' The Doctor knelt over the bed, running the blue light from his sonic screwdriver over the stricken boy.

'What happened?' he asked the friar without looking around. 'The Krashok arrival, what happened?'

Friar Meadows took a deep breath. 'It was a little before dusk. The children playing out near the wheat fields saw what they assumed to be a star glowing brightly and moving in the Eastern sky. At first I dismissed their claims as fictions, a childish game of some kind, but the truth of it...' The friar shook his head. 'The star came low across the fields. The very air seemed to hiss as it passed. Lightning shook the sky, the smell of sulphur engulfed us.'

'That would be the time drive,' the Doctor muttered, more to himself than to anyone else. 'Badly tuned by the sound of things. Tends to stir up the ozone a little.'

Friar Meadows gave the Doctor a wary glance, then continued his tale. 'The star fell on the far side of the castle with a mighty crash, a blaze of light that lit up the sky as if it were midday. We could see the men on Sir Blackheart's battlements pointing at where it lay. I urged the men of our village to have no part in this madness, to stay and protect their homes and families, but the harvest has been poor this year, and the thought of what treasures might be found in a star from the heavens was too much for some.'

'So they went to see what they could find.' The

Doctor's voice was quiet.

'And found nothing but death.'

'You saw what happened?' asked Gisella gently.

The friar nodded. 'A huge ship of metal, half buried in the woodland bordering the castle. Its skin steamed and crackled. I pleaded with the men not to approach, but they were entranced by it, entranced by the promise of treasure from heaven. But this… thing was not from heaven.' He crossed himself. 'The metal cracked open with a blaze of light and the demons stepped out of their fallen star.'

'The Krashoks.' The Doctor's face was grim.

'Call them what you will, they were not of this Earth, of that I am certain. They struck down our men with weapons the like of which I have never seen. Even when the men tried to flee the demons cut them down.' Meadows touched the young man's forehead. 'Ralph had almost reached me when the demon fire engulfed him. I managed to get him back to the church. I returned to recover our dead when night had finally fallen.'

'You're a brave man,' said the Doctor. 'You could have left them.'

'And denied them a Christian burial?' The friar shook his head. 'More than my life is worth, Doctor.'

The boy on the bed groaned.

'Do you know what is wrong with him?' Gisella knelt at the Doctor's side.

'It's tricky,' said the Doctor. 'The Krashoks build weapons, develop weapons, buy weapons, steal weapons, but they've no specific weapon of choice. The villagers could have been cut down by a hundred types of gun from a hundred different worlds. If I can identify the damage that's been caused then I can identify the gun. There's no visible sign of trauma on the bodies so I'm doing progressive internal scans to see if I can find anything anomalous, and then... Aha!'

The Doctor sprang to his feet. 'Got it! It's a sonic disruption! Probably a Martian gun. Explains how he managed to survive! It's a very directional weapon, with a very concentrated narrow beam. He must have been just on the edge of the disruption cone; it's set up a sympathetic resonance in his skeletal structure! I can set up a cancellation wave...' He started adjusting settings on the sonic screwdriver.

'You mean you can cure him?' Oswald stared at him in disbelief.

'Oh yes!' The Doctor twirled the minstrel around. 'Now stand back, there's a good friar. This might set your teeth on edge.'

Activity

Find the wave form that will cancel out the sonic damage to Ralph's body — it will be the exact opposite of the sonic wave embedded in Ralph's bones.

1
2
3
4

The Doctor pressed the stud on the screwdriver and a high pitched trill cut through the air. Oswald gave a cry of pain, clapping his fingers over his ears. Glass rattled in the window frames and from outside there was a sudden flurry of barking from the local dogs.

'Not that one, then,' the Doctor said. 'Better try another frequency. But if I get it wrong this time, it could kill him.' He carefully adjusted the sonic screwdriver, took a deep breath, and tried again.

Again, there was a high-pitched noise. But slowly the piercing whine faded. As it did Ralph's agitated flailing became calmer. The Doctor stuck the screwdriver back in his jacket pocket and again crouched down by the bed.

Friar Meadows stared at him incredulously. 'A miracle.'

'Not really. You just need frequency number two and a bit of luck,' the Doctor said. 'He's a strong lad. But it'll take a few days before he's back on his feet again. Calcium, that's what he needs. Build up that bone structure again. Milk! We need some milk. And cheese. You can't go wrong with a good cheese.'

'We've nothing here, but the inn…'

74

'I'll go.' Gisella looked eagerly at the Doctor. 'I want to help.'

'I will go with you,' said Oswald his eyes full of admiration for what he had just witnessed. 'I wish to help too.'

The Doctor hesitated for a moment, wary of what had nearly happened earlier, then nodded. 'All right.'

Gisella and Oswald hurried to the door.

'But be careful,' the Doctor called after them. Gisella turned and gave him a cheeky grin, then vanished. There was a groan from the bed as Ralph tried to rise.

The Doctor and Friar Meadows hurried over to him. 'It's all right. You're safe. You're fine.'

'The demons?' Ralph looked around fearfully

'Far from here,' said the friar soothingly.

'You're sure?'

'Yes, my son. There is nothing that can harm you here.'

But his words were drowned out by a terrifying scream from outside.

A Knight's Work

At the very second that the Doctor scrambled to his feet the door to the church crashed open and Oswald tumbled inside, slamming the door behind him. From outside came the snort of horses, the sound of running and the frightened cries of women and children.

'What's happening?' The Doctor crossed to the breathless minstrel. 'Where's Gisella?'

'They came out of nowhere.' Oswald stammered. 'We'd barely got halfway across the square…'

'And you left her…' The Doctor's face darkened dangerously.

'We both ran. I couldn't keep up with her…'

The Doctor pushed Oswald to one side, peering through a crack in the door. A dozen armoured men on horseback were clustered in the centre of the village, two of them held blazing torches that cast flickering shadows over the frightened crowd of villagers. The men were heavily armed, though the Doctor was relieved to see that none of them held any Krashok weapons.

As he watched one of the knights swung himself down from his steed. He pulled off his helmet, looking around at the expectant crowd.

'Sir Robert Markham,' whispered Oswald. 'Lord Blackheart's most trusted man.'

'Lord Blackheart needs workers at the castle,' bellowed Markham.

Jacob, the head man, pushed to the front of the crowd, standing defiantly before the towering knight.

'Work that requires you to drag folk from their homes at sundown? What work is so urgent?'

'No concern of yours, Jacob Riley. Just do as you are bid and you will be back in your beds before sunrise.'

Jacob looked over at where Markham's knights were pulling people from their houses. 'You say it as if we had a choice.'

From the far side of the square there was the sound of a scuffle. The Doctor's heart sank as he saw Gisella pulled from behind one of the wooden houses, pushed forward with half a dozen boys and girls of similar age.

Markham nodded. 'Good. Take them and a dozen more.'

Jacob stared at him in disbelief as the children were pushed crying towards the waiting horses.

'What work requires the use of children?'

A look of shame flickered over Markham's face.

'I give you my word, no harm will come to them.'

Jacob hefted the club in his hand.

'Not good enough, Markham. You're not taking our children.'

There was a flash of metal and Jacob's club was swept to the floor. He stared fearfully at the sword that was now pressed to his throat.

'I'm sorry, Jacob,' said Markham. 'But I have my orders.'

He turned to his men. 'Three of you, take them to the castle. The rest, search for this *Doctor*.'

The Doctor watched helplessly as Gisella and the other villagers were bundled out of the village square by Markham's men and herded towards the castle at sword point.

Oswald pulled frantically at the Doctor's arm.

'You must hide!'

'I can't leave Gisella.'

'You are no use to her captured by them!'

Friar Meadows scurried forward. 'Come with me.'

He led the Doctor and Oswald across the church to a carved wooden panel below the simple cross. He ran his fingers around the edge, then pressed hard. There was a click and the panel swung open with a waft of stale air.

'A secret passage?' The Doctor raised a quizzical eyebrow.

'It leads to the lower levels of the castle. It was built as a sanctuary for the nuns who used to worship here, a relic of more dangerous times. It has been sealed for many years...' The friar broke off.

'Something happened?' asked the Doctor gently.

'A terrible crime. Outlaws ran riot, burning and looting. The nuns ran for the church, meaning to take refuge at the castle but a novice, a young girl, panicked, sealed herself behind the door and could not open it again. No one could follow her... No one survived that night. No one save the young girl trapped behind the door, listening to the screams.'

Oswald stared into the dark tunnel. 'And where is the girl now?'

The friar said nothing.

Oswald started to back away. 'Perhaps we should find another hiding place...'

There was the noise of swords being drawn and raised voices from outside.

'Quickly!' Friar Meadows bundled them into the opening, pulling the door shut behind them. The Doctor stared at him anxiously. 'You're not coming with us?'

The friar shook his head. 'I can delay them, you stand more chance if I stay here. Besides...' He shot a look over at the bed where Ralph lay. 'Someone needs to look after poor Ralph. Now go!'

He pushed the door closed. There was a sharp click and the Doctor and Oswald were plunged into darkness.

The Doctor pressed his ear to the wooden panel, listening as the knights barged their way into the church. There was a bellow of anger as the friar protested indignantly that this was a place of God, and the muttered apologies of Markham's men.

The Doctor smiled. He didn't envy them, having to choose between the wrath of their leader or the righteous indignation of the friar. Still, he couldn't imagine that the belligerent friar would stop them searching for long. He shuffled round in the cramped passageway and peered into the gloom.

'So, the good friar says that this tunnel leads all the way to the castle...' he murmured.

'You're not suggesting...' Oswald whispered, his voice wavering.

'Oh yes, Come on, Oswald. Allons-y!'

Gisella pulled her shawl tight over her head as she was led through the main gate of Blackheart's castle. She was still cursing herself that she had been captured so easily, but this time trying to fight her way out against armed men hadn't seemed like the sensible option. Besides, the Doctor had wanted to find a way inside the castle and although this way wasn't ideal, at least she'd managed it.

Despite her situation, she smiled. She doubted that the Doctor would approve of her somewhat unorthodox method of entry.

The ragged crowd of villagers was shepherded through a wide courtyard, the men clustered protectively around the younger children. The children themselves were all being surprisingly calm, as if getting inside the castle was some kind of adventure. But then, so far there had been no sign of the Krashoks. Gisella doubted that things would be so calm when they finally showed up.

They were brought to a halt in front of a wide pair of steps leading up to a set of massive wooden doors. One of the knights climbed the stairs and tentatively eased one of the doors open.

Through the crack Gisela could see flaring electric blue light that came from nothing in this time period. The villagers had noticed it too and began to murmur and back away. A shadow loomed against the light, and with a splintering crash the doors were flung open.

Children screamed as the Krashok stared down at them, lips curled disdainfully over yellowed tusks. With a sinking heart Gisella realized that it was Commander Grelt. She had been standing right in front of him back at the warehouse. If he saw her, he was bound to recognize her.

She pulled her shawl tight around her head as the Krashok Commander started to descend the steps towards her.

Oswald squeezed himself along the dark narrow passage, his cloak snagging on tree roots and sharp stones, mud and slime caking his hands and knees.

They had been crawling for what seemed like hours. Ahead of him he could see the flicker of blue light from the Doctor's magical torch as he pushed on through the seemingly endless dark passage.

'Ah...' The Doctor's voice echoed from in front of him.

'What is it?' asked Oswald, panicking.

'The tunnel seems to branch off three different ways.'

The Doctor shone the blue light ahead of him, illuminating the mouths of three passageways.

'So, which way do you think we should go?'

Oswald didn't think that any of the tunnels looked particularly inviting but said nothing. He nodded at the slim tube in the Doctor's hand. 'Will your magic device not tell us which passage to take?'

The Doctor smiled. 'I wish it could, Oswald. Unfortunately we're just going to have to take pot luck.'

Activity

Which path will lead the Doctor and Oswald in the right direction?

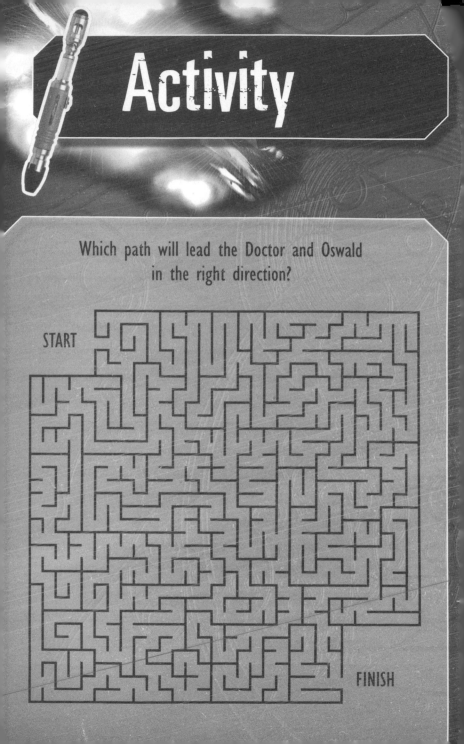

START

FINISH

'Looks like we chose the right passage,' called the Doctor. 'Come and see. Right was right, which sort of makes sense.'

Oswald crawled forward and peered out of the tunnel mouth. The roughly scraped mud walls had opened out into a passageway wide enough for the two of them to stand side-by-side and tall enough for them to stand upright. The Doctor helped him to his feet and Oswald stretched gratefully. 'I was beginning to think I would never be warm again.'

'Yes,' the Doctor frowned. 'It is warm. Too warm. In fact it's *much* too warm! And I can smell something.' His nose wrinkled. ' Can you smell something?'

Oswald sniffed. There was something, a smell like...

'Roasting meat.'

'Yes...' The Doctor played the light from his metal device over the mud walls. Oswald jumped as the blue glow illuminated a shape set into the wall.

'What's that?'

The Doctor wandered over to the shape. 'I don't think we're alone down here,' he murmured.

Oswald hurried over to see what he had found. It was a human skull.

Tunnel Vision

isella stood at the back of the group of cowering villagers trying her best not to make herself conspicuous. The Krashok Commander bellowed his orders at the clearly terrified knights and they ushered the villagers into the great hall of the castle. Gisella was pleased to see the extent of the damage that the Doctor had caused to the Krashok machinery, but her pleasure was short lived when she realized that the Krashok technicians had all but finished their repair work.

A thin, bearded man in long robes stood at the far end of the hall, framed by the vast stone fireplace. Gisella assumed that this was Lord Blackheart. Certainly he was the only human in the room whose clothes weren't stained with oil and grease, and who face was not drawn and grey. Grelt was talking animatedly to him, pointing back at the assembled villagers.

Clearly he wasn't happy about something.

As Gisella watched, Grelt swept his arm across one of the wooden tables sending components crashing to the floor. The sudden noise brought silence to the room. The Krashok stamped across to his men, who all busied themselves with their work.

The villagers shuffled nervously as Blackheart approached them.

'Who speaks for you?'

Jacob shuffled forward, eyes firmly fixed on the floor.

'I do my lord.'

'Has it been explained what is required of you?'

'Only that you need workers, men… and children.'

Blackheart nodded. 'You are to assist in the transportation of these… items.' He gestured to the alien machinery. 'They are to be taken to the creatures' vessel that rests in the eastern meadow. The children are to work inside the vessel as instructed.'

Jacob raised his eyes, staring Blackheart in the face. 'You would send children to do the work of demons? You would send them into their lair? You are our Lord. You are bound to protect us, it is your duty…'

'Do not presume to lecture me on my responsibilities!' snapped Blackheart. 'Be thankful that the creatures are happy for you to work without whips or chains.'

Jacob held his gaze. 'What thrall do these creatures have you under that you forsake both your King and your God?'

Gisella saw uncertainty flicker across Blackheart's face. 'I give you my word that you will not be harmed,' he whispered. 'Do as the creatures bid you. By daybreak I will have completed my side of the bargain, and God willing the demons will give me what I desire and be gone from our land.'

With that he turned and crossed to the great doors, slipping out into the cold night air. Gisella, watching him go, wondered what deal a medieval Lord could possibly have struck with the Krasholm.

Her musing was cut short as Grelt and one of his subordinates crossed to the frightened group, glaring at them balefully.

'Get these primitives to work,' snapped the Krashok Commander. 'I want the main drive circuits reinstalled in the ship within the hour. Markham has failed me, Jorak. You and I will search for the Doctor ourselves.'

The other Krashok looked concerned. 'But Commander, is it wise...'

'I listened to you once, Jorak, I thought your advise sound. It was not. Do not advise me badly again.' Grelt snatched a device from his belt and starting adjusting it with heavy claws. 'Back in the warehouse the Doctor used a sonic device. Such technology is unknown on this planet. We will recalibrate the scanner to detect energy emissions from sophisticated equipment. It will pinpoint the Doctor's position and we will hunt him down.'

Gisella stared in horror at the Krashok Commander. When he activated his device, it would detect the energy emissions from her own robotic body. She was about to be discovered.

The Doctor was beginning to wish that he had left Oswald back at the church with Friar Meadows. The young minstrel was a bundle of nerves, and not for the first time the Doctor found himself wondering what was happening to Gisella.

Having convinced Oswald that they were not in any danger of being eaten by some ravening, man-eating underground monster they had made their way along the ever widening passage. The Doctor had swapped his sonic screwdriver for one of the many candles that they had found stuffed into alcoves in the walls.

A ragged swathe of cloth hung in the passageway ahead of them. The Doctor drew it aside gingerly. The passageway opened out into a wide cavern. The floor was wet and uneven, the sound of dripping water echoing around the gloom. Long thin stalactites hung like petrified vines from the wet rock above them and shadows thrown from the guttering fire in the centre of the cave danced across the walls.

The Doctor was about to investigate the strange cave when a voice rang out through the darkness. 'Witch! Where are you?'

The Doctor pushed Oswald backwards as a man in long dark robes emerged from the cave from another tunnel.

Oswald gripped the Doctor's arm. 'That's Lord Blackheart!' he whispered.

'Is it now…' The Doctor pursed his lips. 'I wonder what he's doing skulking around down here in the dark?'

'Witch! I have summoned you!' Blackheart

bellowed into the gloom once more. 'Do not presume to keep me waiting.'

'I beg your forgiveness, my Lord.' The rasping voice rang out from the gloom. 'These bones do not move as swiftly as they once did.'

Oswald took an involuntary step backwards as an emaciated figure shambled out of the shadows. Even the Doctor found himself flinching as the flickering candlelight illuminated the face before them.

It was impossible to tell how old the woman was. Long, dank strands of hair clung to her skull, draping over her shoulders like seaweed. The tattered remnants of her clothes were dirty and stinking, the dark fabric hanging in ragged strips, barely covering the form beneath. Every inch of exposed skin was a mass of swirling painted symbols, some vivid red and still wet, others dark and crusted. The Doctor had a strong suspicion they had been painted with blood.

Whilst her body was frail and sickly, the woman's eyes blazed with a fierce intelligence. They gleamed from beneath her matted hair as she bowed falteringly before Lord Blackheart.

'My Lord. A pleasure to welcome you to my humble dwelling once more.'

'Cease your mindless flattery. You promised me

94

that these demons would give me what I asked. You foretold it!'

'Indeed, my Lord. By sundown tomorrow these creatures from another time will have reunited you with your dead queen. That is written, it cannot be undone.'

'But the cost! These creatures work my servants till they drop. They take the people from the village. Women and children! Is this too written?'

The witch smiled horribly. 'The price of love is too high for you, Lord Blackheart?'

Blackheart caught hold of the witch by her scrawny neck. 'Let me foretell your future for you. Seeing my beloved rise again is the only thought that keeps me alive, but if one child dies by the hands of these creatures, then I shall see you burn.'

He pushed the woman away, wiping his hands on his cloak in distaste. 'Watch the demons for me. Watch them closely. Send word to me as the time of their departure draws near.'

'As my Lord commands.' The witch turned and shambled to a set of grimy drapes, pulling them aside and revealing yet another passage leading from the cavern. She turned and shot a sly look back at Blackheart. 'By sundown tomorrow my

Lord. All will be as I foretold.' Then she vanished into the dark.

Blackheart turned and swept out from the cavern, candles guttering in his wake. The Doctor stepped into the cavern, waving at Oswald to follow him.

'Quickly, Oswald, we don't have much time.' He pressed his sonic screwdriver into the young minstrel's hand. 'Follow her. If that tunnel leads to the Krashok spacecraft then there's a chance you can find Gisella. When you do, give this sonic screwdriver to her. Tell her to get the villagers free and get away from there.'

'What about you?' asked Oswald. 'Where are you going?'

'I'm going to follow Lord Blackheart. It sounds as though the Krashoks have promised Blackheart the use of the Eternity Crystal. If that's true then I can't let it happen. I'm going to try and tell him what the Krashoks are really like, try and get him to help us.'

'I think I'd rather come with you.' Oswald was looking decidedly pale.

'Listen to me,' the Doctor said urgently. 'The Krashoks aren't known for their hospitality, I doubt very much they're going to wait until people have reached a safe distance before they try and leave. That means a lot of people are going to die.'

Oswald swallowed hard. 'Then I will do my best.'

'Good lad.' The Doctor patted him on the arm. 'Now get after witchy-poo before you lose her.' Oswald hurried down the passageway, sonic screwdriver held out in front of him like a sword.

The Doctor turned and hurried down the passageway after Lord Blackheart. It was time to end this.

Power of the Krashoks

Grelt stopped work on his scanner recalibrations as Markham threw open the doors of the main hall, pulling off his helmet and thrusting it into the arms of a waiting squire.

Grelt smiled unpleasantly as he approached. 'Ah, Sir Knight. Do I gather that your hunt has been unsuccessful?'

'Your Doctor has gone to ground,' growled Markham unhappily. 'I will set out again at first light. We shall take hounds and beaters. We will find him.'

'It seems rash of you to make such bold promises, Markham. "Before this night is out," you told me. I thought you to be a man of your word.'

Markham looked as though he had been struck. His hand reached for the hilt of his sword.

'You dare to impugn my honour, demon?'

'Your honour?' Grelt shook his head, tutting to himself. 'No, Sir Knight, your honour is not of any concern to me, merely your efficiency. We leave this world within the next two cycles. That cannot be delayed whilst we wait for you to accomplish the simple task that you have been set.'

Markham reddened. 'If you wish the job completed with haste then perhaps you should assist us by the means of your magic machines instead of sitting here, mocking us.'

'You are right, Sir Knight.' Grelt nodded slowly. 'I have been unfair.' He handed Markham the tracking device. 'Here. This will take you to whatever hole the Doctor is hiding in.'

Markham took the device, staring uncertainly at the Krashok.

'And for the slur I have cast upon your honour, I shall let you have the pleasure of dispatching him.' Grelt unclipped the blaster from his belt. 'My weapon, Sir Knight, my side of the bargain, in good faith of your task completed.'

Markham took the proffered weapon, his face expressionless. He hefted the gun in his hand, his fingers curling around the grip.

'Thank you, demon. An unexpected gesture.

And one you will regret.'

With one swift movement he stepped back, levelling the gun at the Krashok's head. 'You have blighted my master and this castle with your presence. Return to hell where you belong.'

He pulled the trigger.

There was a sharp click.

Grelt gave a smile that was far too full of teeth to be friendly. 'Bravo, Sir Knight. You are a credit to your Lord and your race. I knew as soon as you had laid eyes on our weapons that you would try and find a way to use them against us if you could. Unfortunately for you, I removed the power pack from that particular weapon, in case of just such... eventualities.'

He pulled a black cylinder from his belt.

'Cyberguns, however, have an inexhaustible power supply. A far more superior hand weapon I think, and one I always recommend to our clients.'

He levelled the cybergun at the dumbfounded knight and pressed the trigger. There was a harsh rattle and smoke curled from inside Sir Markham's armour. His face frozen in an expression of pain and surprise, the knight toppled to the floor with a deafening crash.

Grelt snatched up the tracker and gun from

the lifeless body and stared around the hall at the terrified villagers. 'Let that be a lesson to all of you. I expect my orders to be obeyed. Make no mistake. I am in charge here. You will do as I command, or you will die!'

Blackheart closed the door of his private chapel and sat down heavily on one of the hard wooden pews, his head hung in exhaustion. All his plans, all his dreams were starting to unravel around him. The elation that he had first felt when he had been told that he could bring his beloved Beatrice back from the dead had now faded into a dull dread at the price that her resurrection would cost. He lifted his head and stared at the serene stone features on the tomb he had built for her.

'What would you have me do?' he whispered.

'Getting difficult isn't it?' A voice asked from the shadows.

Blackheart jumped to his feet. A thin man in a long coat stepped out from the behind the pillars.

'Who are you?' He snatched the dagger from his belt, levelling it at the stranger. 'How did you get in here?'

'I'm the Doctor.' The man's voice was low and

calm. 'I followed you from the cave.'

'How dare you enter my private chapel? My servants will have you beaten for this.'

'What and explain to them that I followed you down a secret passage? Have to explain why you visit a secret cave beneath the castle. To visit a *witch*.' The Doctor scratched his chin. 'That's not going to sound very good, is it? Local Lord in Sordid Sorcery Scandal. Tabloids would have a field day with that.'

'So.' Blackheart growled. 'You want coins. Gold to keep your mouth shut.'

'No. I want to stop this. I want to help you. That's all.'

'Help?' Blackheart gave a barking laugh. 'How can you possibly help me?'

'Because I know what the Krashoks are. I know where they come from. I know that they thrive on conflict, that they trade in death for nothing more worthy than their own financial gain. I know that they are responsible for wars and suffering and mayhem across the seven galaxies. I know what it is you've been promised. I know that you hope to raise your wife from the dead and I know why it will never happen. You are a good man, Sir Howard, a man of honour. The Krashoks will take that from you. The life of your wife will be paid for in the blood of innocents.'

Blackheart let the dagger drop slowly. 'How can you know these things?'

'The future, Lord Blackheart. I see the future. I see how you will be remembered in history if you let them do this.'

'But my wife, my Beatrice…'

'Is dead, and I'm sorry. But you can't bring her back.'

'But *they* can!' Blackheart's eyes were pleading. 'Their magic…'

'Is an illusion. The machine they have is not a way of cheating death. It is a way of keeping the dead as living dead. Bringing them back from the battlefield to fight again and again and again. To continue the pain and misery. Please, Lord Blackheart. You must believe me.'

Blackheart turned away. Not wanting to listen to the Doctor's words, but knowing that he must.

The silence was broken as a squire, his face streaked with tears, burst into the chapel.

Blackheart spun. 'What is it? What has happened?'

'Lord Markham,' the squire stammered. 'The

demons. They struck him down. Now they are rounding up everyone they can find and taking them to their vessel.'

Blackheart bowed his head, silent for a moment before the tomb of his dead wife, then he turned to the Doctor, his eyes full of hate and anger.

'Let us send these demons back to hell where they belong.'

For what seemed like hours Oswald had crept along the winding passageway straining to see any sign of the woman ahead of him.

She seemed to move through the narrow muddy tunnels with astonishing agility, slipping past grasping tree roots and jutting boulders with ease. Oswald found himself snagged on every branch and root, every rock and stalactite. His face was scratched and bleeding, his clothes torn and streaked with mud and dirt and he was beginning to think that he would be lost forever in this underground labyrinth.

The passageway suddenly turned abruptly upwards and Oswald felt a cool breeze on his face. The thought of being out in the open again spurred him forwards, pushing through the muddy tunnel before finally tumbling out into the cool night.

He lay on his back panting, drawing in deep lungfuls of air. When his breath had returned he sat up, and his jaw dropped in astonishment at the sight in front of him.

When the Doctor had spoken of the Krashok's ship Oswald hadn't really known what to think. Perhaps another blue box similar to the one he had seen appear from the air. Nothing prepared him for the sight in the clearing below.

The Krashok ship was a vast disc of metal, the curves and vents in the metal skin gleaming under the cold light of the moon. Harsh yellow light spilled from the underbelly of the craft and picked out a ragged line of terrified villagers struggling with heavy equipment under the watchful eyes of the Krashoks.

Oswald cowered backwards at the sight of the towering aliens, the jumble of monstrous features that made up their snarling faces far more terrifying than anything in his wildest imaginings.

As he pulled himself backwards over the frozen grass his hands suddenly touched something greasy and warm.

He turned and found himself staring into the

gaunt painted face of the witch.

With a cry Oswald fumbled for the sonic screwdriver.

The screwdriver gave a high-pitched whine that made Oswald's ears ring. At the same time something grasped him firmly by the shoulders...

To Battle!

Gisella hauled the piece of Krashok machinery that she had been given into the bowels of the ship. She pretended to struggle under the weight when the truth was she could have carried the device in one hand. Around her, the villagers stared in frightened awe at the gleaming surroundings of the Krashok ship. Most of them were unable to comprehend the things they were seeing.

The Krashoks themselves were merciless taskmasters. Beating anyone who stumbled under the weight of their machinery, laughing unpleasantly when their more technical instructions were met with blank incomprehension.

From what Gisella could see the Krashoks had removed their primary drive systems for repair and were now using the forced labour of the villagers to lift the bulky equipment back into place. Gisella could see service robots standing dormant at their recharge stations. Presumably the Krashoks were trying to preserve power until the last possible moment. She and the other children had been separated from the rest of the group and the Krashoks were forcing the smaller ones down the service conduits to connect the power cables.

Gisella gritted her teeth as a crying child was cuffed harshly by a growling Krashok and forced into one of the service conduits. She stared up defiantly at the alien as it crossed to her.

'You will enter the conduit.' It gestured at a narrow space with a serrated claw. 'You will connect the black cables to the sockets you will find. Get it wrong and you will be punished. Do you understand, primitive?'

Gisella nodded and scrambled into the metal tube. She glanced back over her shoulder as the Krashok moved on. Good. That gave her some breathing space.

She looked around, trying to get her bearings. The power couplings were arranged like the spokes of a wheel. At the centre would be the main drive system. If she could get there then she would be able to make her way to any part of the ship. If she could find the Eternity Device with its fake Crystal…

She felt the lump of the *real* Crystal in the folds of her jacket, suddenly realizing that bringing the very thing that the Krashoks were after into the heart of their ship might not have been the wisest decision. She shook her head. There was no choice now.

Around her there was the sound of muffled sobbing. Gisella could see dozens of children wedged into the machinery of the Krashok ship. She couldn't just leave them here.

She twisted round in the narrow space. The power systems of the ship were tremendously volatile. If she was right then there should be an emergency system.

A vent in the floor caught her eye and she smiled. 'Perfect.'

The Krashok ship had an emergency venting system for releasing dangerous plasma in the event of an engine malfunction. It would lead to the hull of the ship and outside. But she had to open it without setting off the emergency alarms.

There was a panel set into the wall.

Activity

What set of 3 symbols are repeated twice in this sequence?

♥♥8M♥M8MM8♥M8

1 = M
2 = ♥
3 = 8

ANSWER

She pressed the final symbol and the grill swung inwards revealing a long sloping shaft. It was easy really, once she had realized that the three symbols were just numbers – numbers reflected and copied so that one looked like a letter M, and two like a heart, and three became eight...

There was a child in the next conduit, a boy watching Gisella with frightened eyes. 'What are you doing?'

'Getting you out of here. Tell the others.'

'But the monsters. If we don't do the tasks they have set us...'

'Let me worry about that, now get the others! Quickly!'

The boy nodded, and hurried away. Soon he was back, followed by more children.

One by one the children squeezed their way through the tangle of machinery and started to slide down the emergency shaft. As soon as the last one had gone Gisella started to move from machine to machine, connecting cables with breathtaking speed. The last thing that she wanted was to stop the Krashoks from leaving earth.

As she connected the final power cable she heard the rough growl of a Krashok from the corridor below. It was Jorak, Grelt's second in command.

'Commander. The tracker has located a non terrestrial power signature.'

Gisella's heart sank as Grelt gave a hiss of satisfaction. They had found her.

'A sonic device. Very close to this ship.'

'Then perhaps I will get satisfaction before I leave, Jorak. Come.'

Gisella listened with disbelief as the two Krashok lumbered away. Their tracker hadn't detected her at all. They had locked in on a sonic device. And that could only be the Doctor!

'Playing with sonic technology can be very dangerous if you don't know what you're doing!'

The Doctor plucked the sonic screwdriver from Oswald's hand, staring down at him sternly. 'I thought I told you that this was to be used in emergencies only.'

'But, I thought…' Oswald stammered.

'He thought that I was a danger to him.' The witch smiled revealing crooked teeth.

'And are you?'

'It is not me you should be worried about, time traveller. It is them.' The witch stretched out a wizened hand. Below them in the clearing Grelt stepped from the hatchway of his ship, weapon raised, the red light from the laser sight on his helmet stabbing out through the night air.

Oswald ducked as a bolt of energy sizzled overhead.

'God preserve us! He means to kill us!'

'Yes,' said the Doctor. 'So it seems. Fortunately I've made a few allies.'

Grelt snapped another round home into the Magnatarri hunting rife and threw it to his shoulder again. All around him the prisoners from the village ran for cover but Grelt had only one person on his mind. He lined up the sights on the Doctor standing up on the hillside.

The Doctor looked straight at him.

And smiled.

As Grelt's finger tightened on the trigger a low rumble shook the ground. His aim spoilt, Grelt turned in frustration and his eyes widened in astonishment.

From across the clearing a dozen knights, their armour gleaming in the moonlight, charged towards the ship on steaming, snorting horses. Grelt barely had time to throw himself to one side as a sword slashed down at him. He rolled to one side bellowing for his men as the knights wheeled about and came at the ship again.

Oswald looked up at the Doctor in disbelief.

'You have sent men on horseback against the demons with magic weapons? You have sent them to their deaths!'

'Except that Lord Blackheart has been very, very co-operative,' the Doctor grinned. 'He told me where the passageway you were in emerged, he's lent me his knights, and he's given me this.'

He held up a small silver box. 'A communicator set to the Krashok frequency, and if I do this...' he pressed the sonic screwdriver into the box. 'Then it should give our friends down there quite a headache.'

He pressed the trigger.

Commander Grelt had the leading knight in his sights when his ears were filled with a deafening, piercing shriek that felt as though it would shatter his skull.

He dropped to his knees, tearing at the helmet grafted to his head. All around he could see villagers fleeing for safety and his men reeling in agony. As he watched two of them were cut down by the swords of the knights, the others turning on their heels and retreating towards the safety of the ship.

He staggered to his feet, his vision blurred from the agonizing noise in his head. In front of him he could see a huge dark shape bearing down on him, the sound of hoof beats reverberating around him. With superhuman effort he grasped the communication pod that bulged from one side of his headset and tore it off, bellowing in pain as it ripped away from his scalp.

The knight looming over him pulled off his helmet.

'Blackheart!' hissed the Krashok.

'You have defiled the memory of my beloved, demon. Now I will send you back from whence you came.'

Blackheart raised his sword, his face filled with hate. Grelt pulled the assembly cybergun from his belt and there was a harsh rattle and a blaze of light.

With a last venomous look at the figure that stared down at him from the hillside, Grelt turned and vanished into his ship.

The Doctor watched in despair as the distant figure of Lord Blackheart toppled from his horse, smoke curling from his armour, crashing to the floor in a crumpled pile.

The witch shuffled forward, wrapping her ragged clothes around her as the wind sent a flurry of snow across the hillside. 'And so the demon has reunited Lord Blackheart with his Queen, just as the writings foretold.'

The Doctor thrust his sonic screwdriver into his jacket pocket. 'I must find Gisella. She's down there somewhere.'

'Too late, Time Lord. The demons have completed their tasks.'

Blue lightning crackled in the winter air, lighting up the clouds and sending tendrils of energy dancing across the treetops.

'No, no, no!' The Doctor could only watch in horror as the Krashok ship faded into nothingness.

'They've gone.' Oswald shook his head in disbelief. 'The demons have gone.'

'Yes,' said the Doctor, his face grim. 'With Gisella trapped on board. And she has the real Eternity Crystal. If they find her then they find it.'

'What will you do?'

'Follow them. Try and catch up with them before they discover her.'

'But how will you know where they have gone?'

The Doctor shook his head. 'I don't know.'

A cry of pain made him turn. The witch had dropped to her knees, her eyes rolled back into her skull showing nothing but white, her body shaking in violent spasms.

The Doctor knelt before her as the shaking stopped. The witch's eyes snapped open. 'The demons have returned to the time from whence they came. Here they used the bodies of our children for their deeds, now they seek those with the keenest minds. Find the brightest of the young, Time Lord, and you will find your friend.'

'The brightest of the young? What does that mean?' The Doctor gripped her by the shoulders. 'Tell me!'

The witch shook her head. 'The writings tell me nothing more.' She hung her head, exhausted by her vision.

The Doctor stood, turning to Oswald. 'Will you take her back to the church, to Friar Meadows? Tell him that his novice needs somewhere better than a cave to live. That her mental gifts need a better outlet than telling the future for a few rich nobles.'

Oswald nodded. 'I won't see you again, will I Doctor?'

The Doctor shrugged. 'Who knows Oswald. Perhaps when you are the greatest bard in all of England I'll come back and watch a gig. Backstage pass of course!'

The Doctor turned and made his way up the hillside, vanishing through the snow covered trees towards his waiting ship. Oswald watched him go. Already he had the making of a poem so epic that it would mark him down as having one of the foremost imaginations in the land.

All he had to work out now was how much he dared to tell.

To be concluded...

To find out what events lie in store for the Doctor and the mystery of the Darksmith Legacy, look out for The End of Time.

But for now, here is a taste of things to come...

BB
DOCTOR·WHO
Book
10
THE DARKSMITH LEGACY
THE END OF TIME
BY JUSTIN RICHARDS
www.thedarksmithlegacy.com
Continue the amazing adventure online...

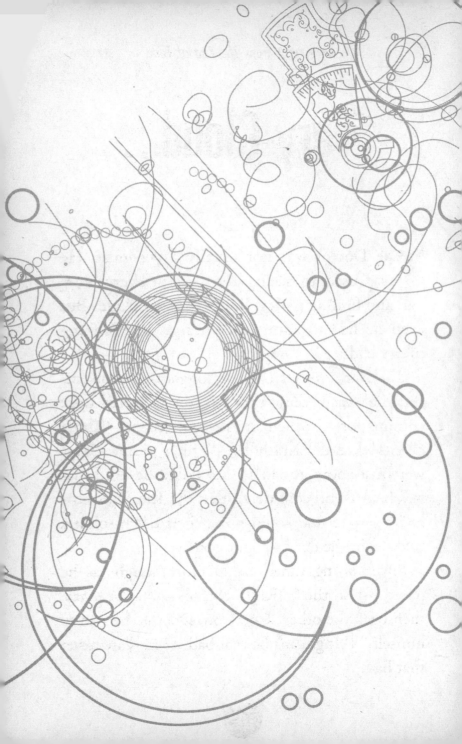

Every Cloud...

The Doctor was not usually a pessimist. He was used to seeing the best in everything, and finding a silver lining to every cloud. But even he had to admit that things were looking pretty bad.

The Darksmiths might no longer be a problem. But that was because they'd finally delivered their commission to their mysterious clients. Those clients were the Krashoks – which meant things were just about as bad as they could be. And that was before you considered that the Krashoks now had a device that could bring their fallen soldiers back from the dead to fight again.

Silver lining time, the Doctor thought as he paced round the TARDIS console – first one way, then back the other. 'Come on, Doctor,' he said to himself. 'Things can't be that bad. Things are never that bad.'

The Krashoks might have the Eternity Device, but Gisella had sabotaged it. She had replaced the all-important Eternity Crystal with a fake, a copy. That was why the Doctor and Gisella had to stop the Krashoks using the device on Earth, because it would have exploded and taken planet Earth with it. They'd succeeded too – so there was another good thing.

But now the Krashoks had gone, and Gisella was with them and the Doctor had no way of knowing where their ship was headed, apart from a cryptic message from a medieval witch.

'Every silver lining has a cloud,' the Doctor decided.

This particular cloud was a thunder cloud if ever there was one. Not only was Gisella trapped on the Krashok ship, but she had the real Eternity Crystal with her. The Doctor had to assume the Krashoks would find Gisella. And when they found her, they would search her and find the Crystal. And when they found the Crystal they would realize the one they had was a fake, and they'd replace it with the real one, and activate their Eternity Device and bring back from the dead every Krashok soldier who had ever lived and died…

Except…

The Doctor paused in mid-step. He slowly put his foot down, carefully so as not to disturb the thought he was in the middle of having.

Why hadn't they activated the Eternity Device already?

They had been short of power after their ship temporally shifted from medieval times back to the present day. But they couldn't pull that trick again. They were stuck in their own zone now – which narrowed things down. And their ship had powered up again and taken off. So now they had the energy to activate the device. But they hadn't done it.

Why not? What did they still need? 'The brightest of the young'? What could that mean?

'Think, Doctor. Think!'

He went through the process in his mind, pretending he was a Krashok. He had the device, ready and primed and calibrated so that it would only revive Krashoks. Otherwise it would bring back every life form that had ever died – like the dead of Mordane. Or even animate and give life to stuff that had never been alive at all. Like the dust on the moon.

Calibrated.

Maybe that was it. It was a faint hope, but a hope nonetheless.

DOCTOR · WHO

THE DARKSMITH LEGACY

'Collected' Party

Celebrate the epic Darksmith Legacy experience with an out-of-this-world party to be held in a secret London location during the October half-term 2009, after the final exciting instalment has been published.

For your chance to win an exclusive ticket to this Doctor Who Extravaganza you must sign up at www.thedarksmithlegacy.com, complete the quest online and submit your details. We will let you know if you have been successful via email.

This will be a once in a lifetime opportunity to win lots of Doctor Who prizes and see scary monsters up-close...

...Don't miss out!

More party details will be revealed in another dimension on the Darksmith website so keep checking back for further updates. Full Terms and Conditions can also be found at www.thedarksmithlegacy.com.